King Jack
and the
Dragon

For Theo, alias King Jack, and his den-building friends – P.B.

For Jesse – H.O.

PUFFIN BOOKS

UK | USA | Canada | Ireland | Australia | India | New Zealand | South Africa

Puffin Books is part of the Penguin Random House group of companies
whose addresses can be found at global.penguinrandomhouse.com.

www.penguin.co.uk   www.puffin.co.uk   www.ladybird.co.uk

Penguin
Random House
UK

First published 2011
This edition published 2012
003

Text copyright © Peter Bently, 2011
Illustrations copyright © Helen Oxenbury, 2011
The moral right of the author/illustrator has been asserted

Printed in China

The authorized representative in the EEA is Penguin Random House Ireland
Morrison Chambers, 32 Nassau Street, Dublin D02 YH68

A CIP catalogue record for this book is available from the British Library

ISBN: 978–0–723–29846–5

All correspondence to:
Puffin Books, Penguin Random House Children's
One Embassy Gardens, 8 Viaduct Gardens, London SW11 7BW

MIX
Paper from
responsible sources
FSC
www.fsc.org   FSC® C018179

King Jack
and the
Dragon

PETER BENTLY & HELEN OXENBURY

PUFFIN

Jack, Zak and Caspar
were making a den,
a mighty great fort for King Jack and his men.

A big cardboard box,

an old sheet and some sticks,

a couple of bin bags,
    a few broken bricks.

A fine royal throne
from a ragged old quilt,

a drawbridge,

a flag,

and the castle
was built.

"Prepare to do battle, brave knights!"
cried King Jack.
"Protect your king's castle
from dragon attack!"

They spent the whole day . . .

fighting dragons . . .

and beasts . . .

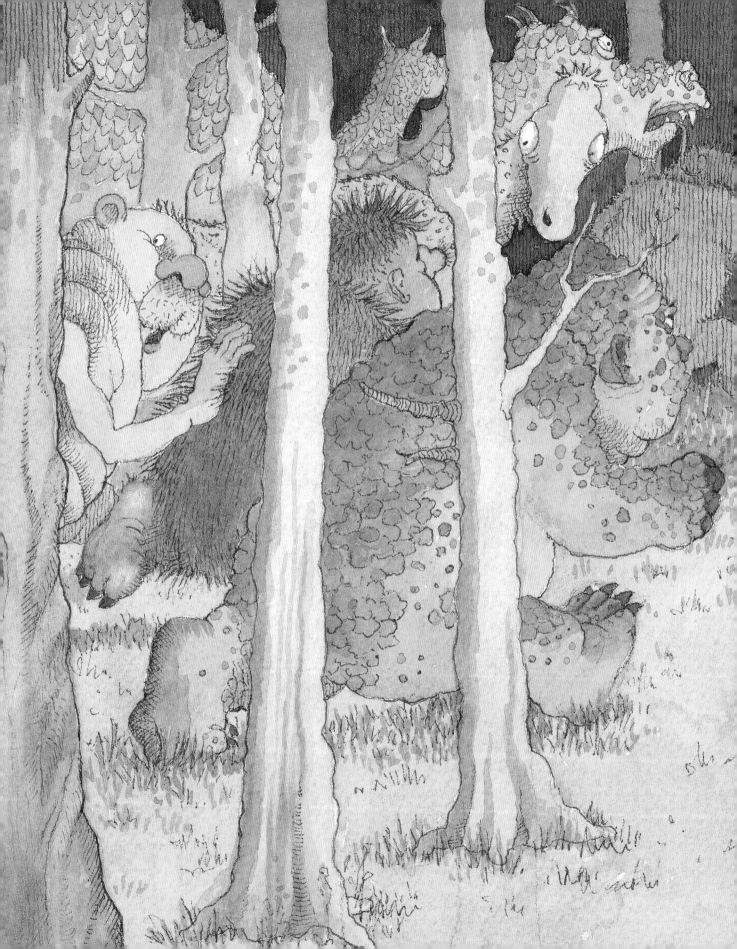

. . . and returned to their stronghold
for fabulous feasts.
"We'll all sleep the night
in the fort," said King Jack.

Then a giant came by
and went home
with Sir Zak.

"Two can fight dragons,
no problem," Jack said . . .

Then another giant came
and took Caspar to bed.

Wrapped up in his blanket,
  Jack sat on his throne.
"All right then," he said. "I'll fight dragons alone."

Then a strong gust of wind
  made the trees start to quiver.
"It's nothing," thought Jack, with a hint of a shiver.

A mouse scampered over the roof,
skitter-scurry.
"It's nothing!" thought Jack.
"There's no reason to worry."

"BRRUP!" croaked a frog.
"It's nothing!" thought Jack,
as he switched on his torch in the deepening black.

"ToO-WhoO!" called an owl. "It's nothing!" Jack said,
as he pulled up his blanket right over his head.

Then
suddenly
brave King Jack's heart
skipped a beat.

He could hear something coming –

a THING
with four feet!

It was outside the drawbridge.

King Jack gave a yelp,

"A dragon! A dragon!

Mum! Dad! Help!"

He wished he was anything else but a king,
as the drawbridge fell open and there stood . . .

the **THING!**

"We're sorry," smiled Mum, "if we gave you a fright.
    But it's time for brave kings to come in for the night."
"And kings who've fought dragons all day
      need a bath,"
said Dad, as he lifted King Jack
    off the path.

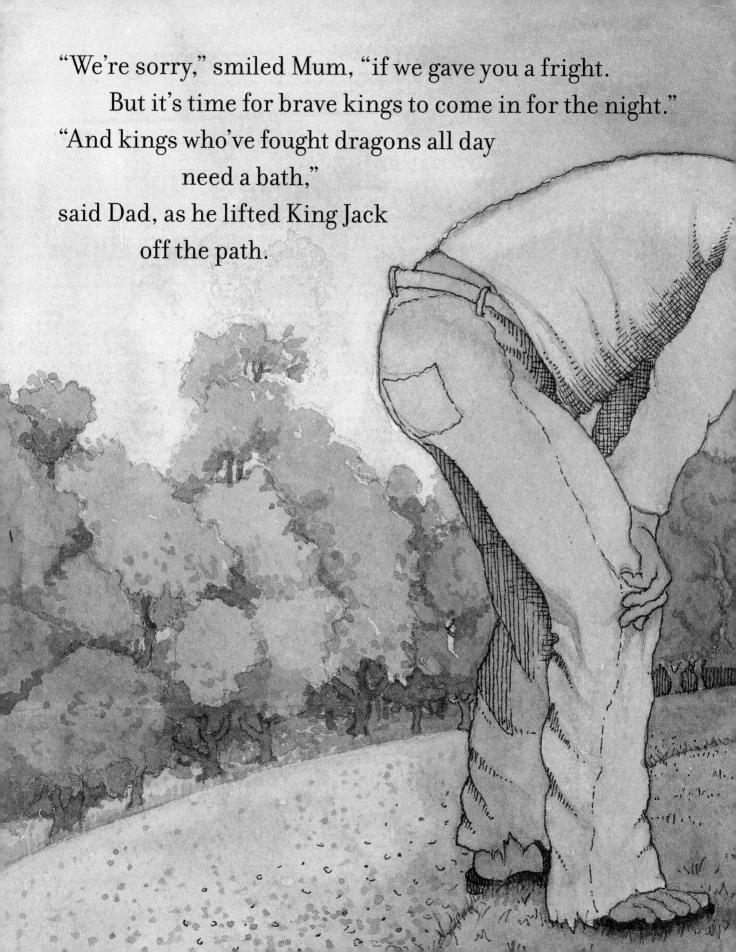

"I knew you weren't really a dragon,"
yawned Jack,
as he bravely rode home on a big giant's back.